D1450564

Dear Parent:
Your child's love of reading starts here!

Every child learns to read in a different way and at his or her own speed. Some go back and forth between reading levels and read favorite books again and again. Others read through each level in order. You can help your young reader improve and become more confident by encouraging his or her own interests and abilities. From books your child reads with you to the first books he or she reads alone, there are I Can Read Books for every stage of reading:

SHARED READING
Basic language, word repetition, and whimsical illustrations, ideal for sharing with your emergent reader

BEGINNING READING
Short sentences, familiar words, and simple concepts for children eager to read on their own

READING WITH HELP
Engaging stories, longer sentences, and language play for developing readers

READING ALONE
Complex plots, challenging vocabulary, and high-interest topics for the independent reader

ADVANCED READING
Short paragraphs, chapters, and exciting themes for the perfect bridge to chapter books

I Can Read Books have introduced children to the joy of reading since 1957. Featuring award-winning authors and illustrators and a fabulous cast of beloved characters, I Can Read Books set the standard for beginning readers.

A lifetime of discovery begins with the magical words "I Can Read!"

Visit www.icanread.com for information
on enriching your child's reading experience.

For Aja and her parents
—J.P.

For Lynn Smith
—Y.A.

HarperCollins®, 🏫®, and I Can Read Book® are trademarks of HarperCollins Publishers.

Library of Congress Cataloging-in-Publication Data
Prelutsky, Jack.
　My parents think I'm sleeping : poems / by Jack Prelutsky ; pictures by Yossi Abolafia. Abolafia, Yossi, ill.— 1st ed.
　　p.　cm.
　Summary: A collection of humorous poems about bedtime.
　ISBN 978-0-06-053720-3 (trade bdg.) — ISBN 978-0-06-053721-0 (lib. bdg.) — ISBN 978-0-06-053722-7 (pbk.)
　[1. Sleep—Juvenile poetry. 2. Children's poetry, American. 3. Sleep—Poetry. 4. American poetry.]
PS3566.R36 M9　1985　　　　　　　　　　　　　　　　　　　　　　　　　　2006019546
811'.54—dc22　　　　　　　　　　　　　　　　　　　　　　　　　　　　　　　　　CIP
　　　　　　　　　　　　　　　　　　　　　　　　　　　　　　　　　　　　　　　AC

❖

Originally published by Greenwillow Books, an imprint of HarperCollins Publishers, in 1985.

I Can Read!™

READING
3
ALONE

My Parents Think I'm Sleeping

poems by **Jack Prelutsky**
Children's Poet Laureate

pictures by **Yossi Abolafia**

HarperCollins*Publishers*

Contents

My Parents Think I'm Sleeping

My parents think I'm sleeping,
but I'm positively not,
for beneath my pile of covers
I am doing quite a lot.

I am reading poems and stories
(I have got my flashlight lit),
I am playing with the pieces
of my model rocket kit.

I was quiet as my shadow
till the moment they were gone,
then I dove beneath the covers
and I snapped my flashlight on.

So my parents think I'm sleeping,
but that's simply their mistake,
I have got them fooled completely,
I am really wide-awake.

Tonight Is
Impossibly Noisy

Tonight is impossibly noisy,
it's filled with a horrible sound,
as if dozens of ogres and tigers
are stuck on a merry-go-round.

It sounds like a monkey battalion
is dancing on needles and pins,
or an out-of-tune elephant orchestra
is sawing on steel violins.

Tonight is impossibly noisy,
the air's full of screeches and roars,
it sounds as if pigs are stampeding,
pursued by enraged dinosaurs.

It sounds like a poltergeist army
is holding a midnight parade,
but it's only the alley cat chorus
in a brassy backyard serenade.

The Clouds I Watched
This Afternoon

The clouds I watched this afternoon
were flocks of silent sheep,
but now they've turned to smoky wolves
that watch *me* while I sleep.

All night they prowl before the moon,

till morning, when I rise,

then once again white fleecy sheep

will float across the skies.

Night Is Here

Night is here, and night is there,
and night is all around,
I feel its presence everywhere,
and yet it makes no sound.

And so it's time to close my eyes
and dream the night away,
until the sun lights up the skies,
and welcomes back the day.

A Spooky Sort of Shadow

There's a spooky sort of shadow

dancing weirdly on the wall,

it's a creature that

I've never seen before.

It's creepy, and it's eerie,

and so positively tall,

that it stretches from

the ceiling to the floor.

Its mouth is full of needles,

and it has a giant eye,

and it's moving

in a hungry sort of way.

It surely could destroy me

if it only cared to try,

so I hope it's had enough

to eat today.

That shadow makes me nervous,
I don't dare to close my eyes,
I'm afraid I may be eaten,
head and all—
if I fall asleep tonight,
I'll be taken by surprise
by that shadow dancing
on my bedroom wall.

What Happens to the Colors?

What happens to the colors
when night replaces day?
What turns the wrens to ravens,
the trees to shades of gray?

Who paints away the garden
when the sky's a sea of ink?
Who robs the sleeping flowers
of their purple and their pink?

What makes the midnight clover
quiver black upon the lawn?
What happens to the colors?
What brings them back at dawn?

I Have Been in Bed
for Hours

I have been in bed for hours,
but I'm sure I'm wide-awake,
for my head is filled with visions
of a forest by a lake.

I hear frogs and crickets calling,

I'm aware of fireflies,

I can see the moon reflected

in an owl's unblinking eyes.

I tiptoe very softly

past a hive of drowsy bees,

high above, a cloud meanders,

tiny stars shine through the trees.

I sit beside the water

as a silent swan glides by,

I climb a breezy hilltop,

where I almost touch the sky.

I watch the fishes splashing
in a clear and crystal stream,
it's a very lovely forest,
far too real to be a dream.

Chocolate Cake

I am lying in the darkness

with a smile upon my face,

as I'm thinking of my stomach,

which has got an empty space,

and that corner of the kitchen

with the piece of chocolate cake

I have got to get my hands on

for my empty stomach's sake.

When my parents both are sleeping

(I can tell by Father's snore),

I will sneak out of my bedroom,

I will tiptoe past their door,

I will slip into the kitchen

without any noise or light,

and if I'm really careful,

I will have that cake tonight.

Rain

I was having trouble sleeping
when I heard the pleasant sound
of raindrops softly falling
on the rooftop and the ground.

I hurried to the window

just to watch them as they fell,

they filled the night with sparkles,

and a fresh and lovely smell.

I started feeling sleepy

so I climbed back into bed,

and fell asleep while listening

to the raindrops overhead.

It Is So Still

It is so still, so still tonight,
there is no sound at all,
no tapping on a windowpane,
no footsteps in the hall,

34

no barking dog or screeching cat,

no mouse beneath my bed,

no rustle of a windy leaf,

no raindrops overhead.

I lie beneath my covers

with my pillow to my ear,

and my breathing and my heartbeat

are the only sounds I hear.

If It Was Sunlight Shining

If it was sunlight shining,
I'd know that it was day,
I'd gobble down my breakfast,
then hurry out to play.

If it was sunlight shining,

I would not be indoors,

I'd race around the garden,

I'd fill the air with roars.

If it was sunlight shining,

I'd be a chimpanzee,

I'd run, I'd jump, I'd tumble,

I'd clamber up a tree.

But it is moonlight shining,
my eyes are getting red,
my head is full of cobwebs,
and I am off to bed.

When I'm Very Nearly Sleeping

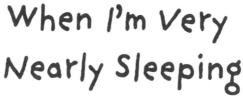

When I'm very nearly sleeping

in the middle of the night,

and I hear the furtive creeping

of a thing that likes to bite,

you may be completely certain

that I haven't any fear,

though when it is on the curtain,

how I wish it were not here.

When I sense the creature perching

on my pillow underneath,

and suspect that it is searching

for a spot to sink its teeth,

when I'm sure I feel it flitting

but an inch above my head,

I am glad a lamp is sitting

on the table by my bed.

A Million Candles

A million candles fill the night,
they glister in the dark,
and though by day they hide their glow,
now each displays its spark.

Amidst them all, there is one light
hat has a special shine,
nd that's the one whose name I know...
think that it knows mine.

I'm Awake!
I'm Awake!

I'm awake! I'm awake!
I cannot shut my eyes,
I'm unable to sleep,
though I've made many tries,

I'm sure I've explored
every inch of my bed,
my body's exhausted,
and so is my head.

I wiggle, I fidget,

I tumble, I twist,

I pound my poor pillow

with fist after fist,

I stopped counting sheep

when I reached ninety-three.

I'm awake! I'm awake!

I cannot fall aslee e e e e e e e e e e e e e e e e e e e e